Dear Parents:

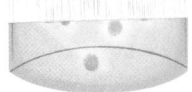

Congratulations! Your child is taking the first steps on an exciting journey. The destination? Independent reading!

STEP INTO READING® will help your child get there. The program offers five steps to reading success. Each step includes fun stories and colorful art or photographs. In addition to original fiction and books with favorite characters, there are Step into Reading Non-Fiction Readers, Phonics Readers and Boxed Sets, Sticker Readers, and Comic Readers—a complete literacy program with something to interest every child.

Learning to Read, Step by Step!

Ready to Read   Preschool–Kindergarten
• big type and easy words • rhyme and rhythm • picture clues
For children who know the alphabet and are eager to begin reading.

Reading with Help   Preschool–Grade 1
• basic vocabulary • short sentences • simple stories
For children who recognize familiar words and sound out new words with help.

Reading on Your Own   Grades 1–3
• engaging characters • easy-to-follow plots • popular topics
For children who are ready to read on their own.

Reading Paragraphs   Grades 2–3
• challenging vocabulary • short paragraphs • exciting stories
For newly independent readers who read simple sentences with confidence.

Ready for Chapters   Grades 2–4
• chapters • longer paragraphs • full-color art
For children who want to take the plunge into chapter books but still like colorful pictures.

STEP INTO READING® is designed to give every child a successful reading experience. The grade levels are only guides; children will progress through the steps at their own speed, developing confidence in their reading. The F&P Text Level on the back cover serves as another tool to help you choose the right book for your child.

Remember, a lifetime love of reading starts with a single step!

To Diane, Gerry, and Aaron
—R.S.

To my wonderful, supportive family
—J.G.

Text copyright © 2021 by Rebecca Smallberg
Cover art and interior illustrations copyright © 2021 by Jessica Gibson

Visit us on the Web!
StepIntoReading.com
rhcbooks.com

Educators and librarians, for a variety of teaching tools, visit us at RHTeachersLibrarians.com

Library of Congress Cataloging-in-Publication Data
Names: Smallberg, Rebecca, author. | Gibson, Jessica, illustrator.
Title: The firefly with no glow / by Rebecca Smallberg ; illustrated by Jessica Gibson.
Description: First edition. | New York : Random House Children's Books, [2021] |
Series: Step into reading ; step 2 | Audience: Ages 4–6. | Audience: Grades K–1. |
Summary: Luke the firefly has no glow of his own so he stays near his friends, and when they are caught in a jar, his difference makes him uniquely qualified to help.
Identifiers: LCCN 2020031650 | ISBN 978-0-593-18134-8 (trade paperback) |
ISBN 978-1-63565-367-0 (library binding) | ISBN 978-1-63565-368-7 (ebook)
Subjects: CYAC: Fireflies—Fiction. | Individuality—Fiction. | Friendship—Fiction.
Classification: LCC PZ7.1.S59434 Fir 2021 | DDC [E]—dc23

Printed in the United States of America   10 9 8 7 6 5 4 3
First Edition

This book has been officially leveled by using the F&P Text Level Gradient™ Leveling System.

The Firefly with No Glow

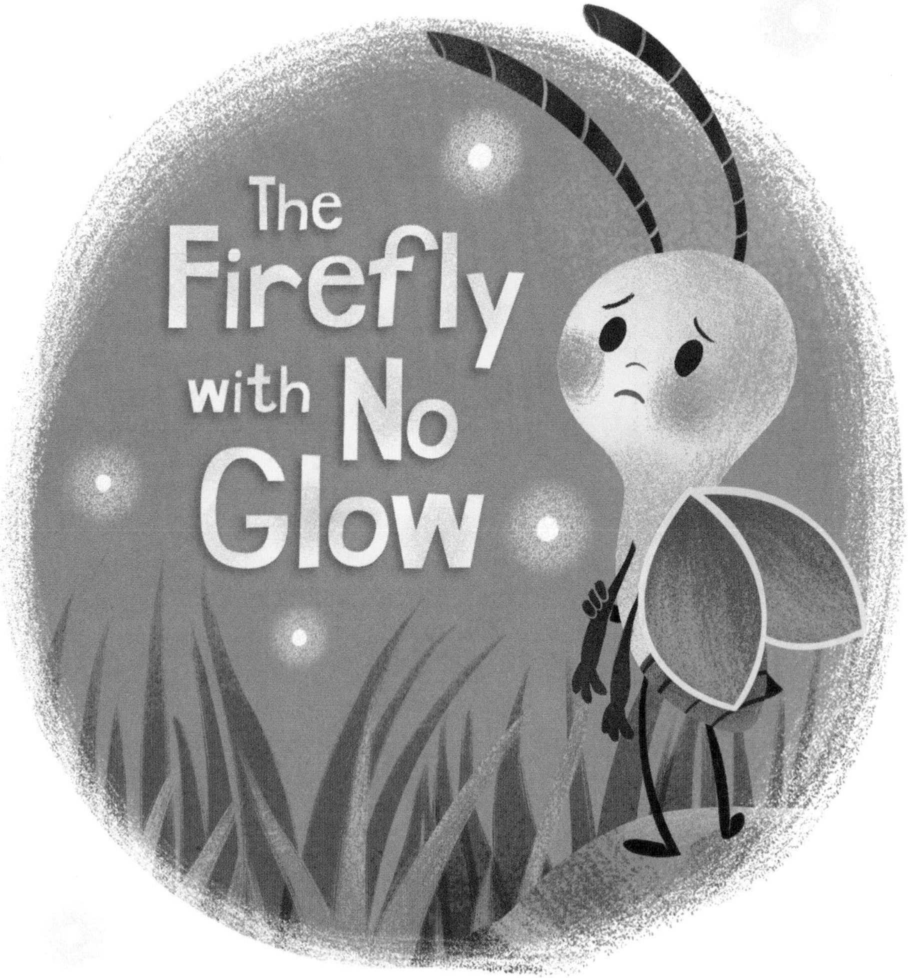

by Rebecca Smallberg
illustrated by Jessica Gibson

Random House 🏠 New York

Luke is a firefly.
He lives in a garden
with snails, spiders,
and other bugs.

The butterflies have
great big wings.
The fireflies have
great big lights.

But Luke does not have
a light of his own.

No light means
no glow.

So Luke stays close
to his friends.

They help him find his
way in the dark.

Luke and his friends
love to explore.

They like
to taste the
sweet flowers.

They like
to smell the
fresh grass.

They like to look up
at the night sky.

Luke likes to count
the shining stars.
Ten stars twinkle
in the night.

The fireflies'
favorite thing to do
is to blink to each other.

Ten fireflies blink
in the dark.
But not Luke.

Luke sees a boy.
The boy is laughing
and dancing.

Luke has never seen
a boy up close before.

His friends

want to go closer.

They fly toward the
boy's sparkling eyes.

They fly in front of his
shiny white teeth.

Just then,
the boy catches a few
of Luke's friends.

Oh no!

They are trapped in a jar.

One of the fireflies
tries to help.

But she gets
caught.

More fireflies come
to help.

The boy chases
their bright lights.

All of them are caught!

Except for Luke.

The boy does not
see him because
Luke has no light.
Maybe Luke can help!

Luke takes a
deep breath.
He flies closer
to the jar.

The boy puts the jar down.
The lid is not closed
all the way.

Luke pulls the
lid up

and up

and up.

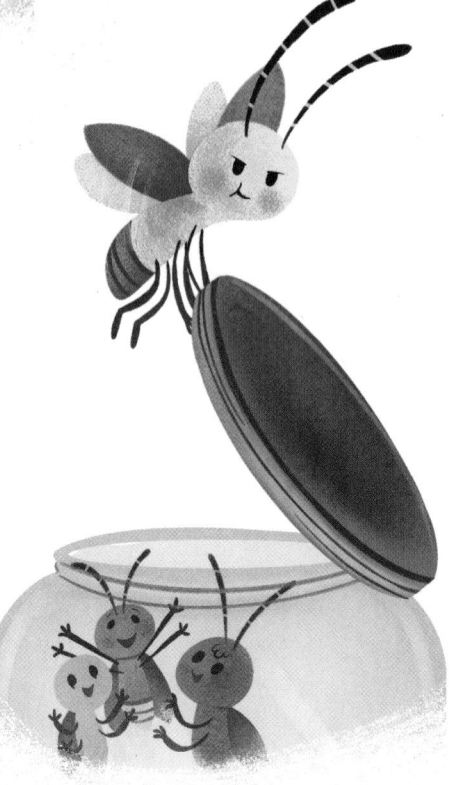

His friends
fly free!

"Luke, you saved us!"
they shout.
"You are a hero!"

Luke and his friends
are glowing.

Yes, even Luke glows now.

Luke is glowing
with pride.